For Emma Blackburn
S.M.

For Amelia
R.A.

B‖F‖&‖F

BRUBAKER, FORD & FRIENDS

AN IMPRINT OF THE TEMPLAR COMPANY LIMITED

A BRUBAKER, FORD & FRIENDS BOOK,
an imprint of The Templar Company Limited

First published in the UK in 2015 by Templar Publishing
This paperback edition published in the UK in 2015 by Templar Publishing,
part of the Bonnier Publishing Group,
The Plaza, 535 King's Road, London, SW10 0SZ
www.templarco.co.uk
www.bonnierpublishing.com

ISBN 978-1-78370-126-1 HARDBACK
ISBN 978-1-78370-127-8 PAPERBACK

Printed in Lithuania

WHOOPS!

SUZI MOORE

illustrated by
RUSSELL AYTO

This is the cat
who didn't know how,
she didn't know
how to say MEOW.

This is the dog
who couldn't bow-wow.
He couldn't say WOOF.
He didn't know how.

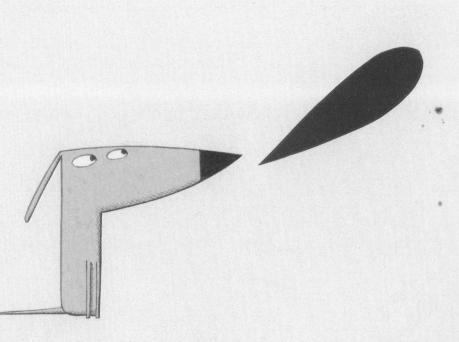

This is the mouse
who just couldn't speak.
She tried very hard
but she couldn't say
SQUEAK!

"Find the old lady at the tumbledown house,"
said the owl to the cat and the dog and the mouse.

"She'll have a spell
to make you all well."

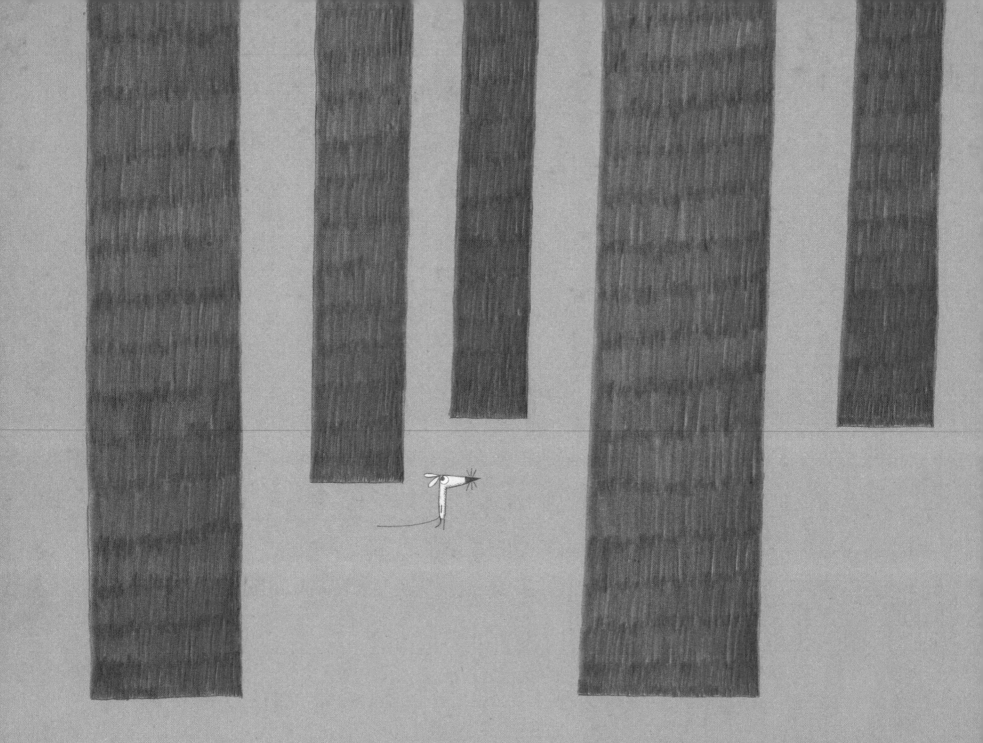

So, they went down the lane and they went through a wood.

The mouse would have squeaked, if only she could.

At the heart of the wood was the tumbledown house.

So in went the cat and the dog and the mouse.

The little old lady, on seeing the three,

said, "I've heard of your problem.

Oh yes, deary me!

Let me find you a spell

to make you all well."

She went to look at her big spell book.

She cast a spell but the whole house shook.

Then the wind blew in.

And the rain came down.

And the tumbledown house
turned round and round.

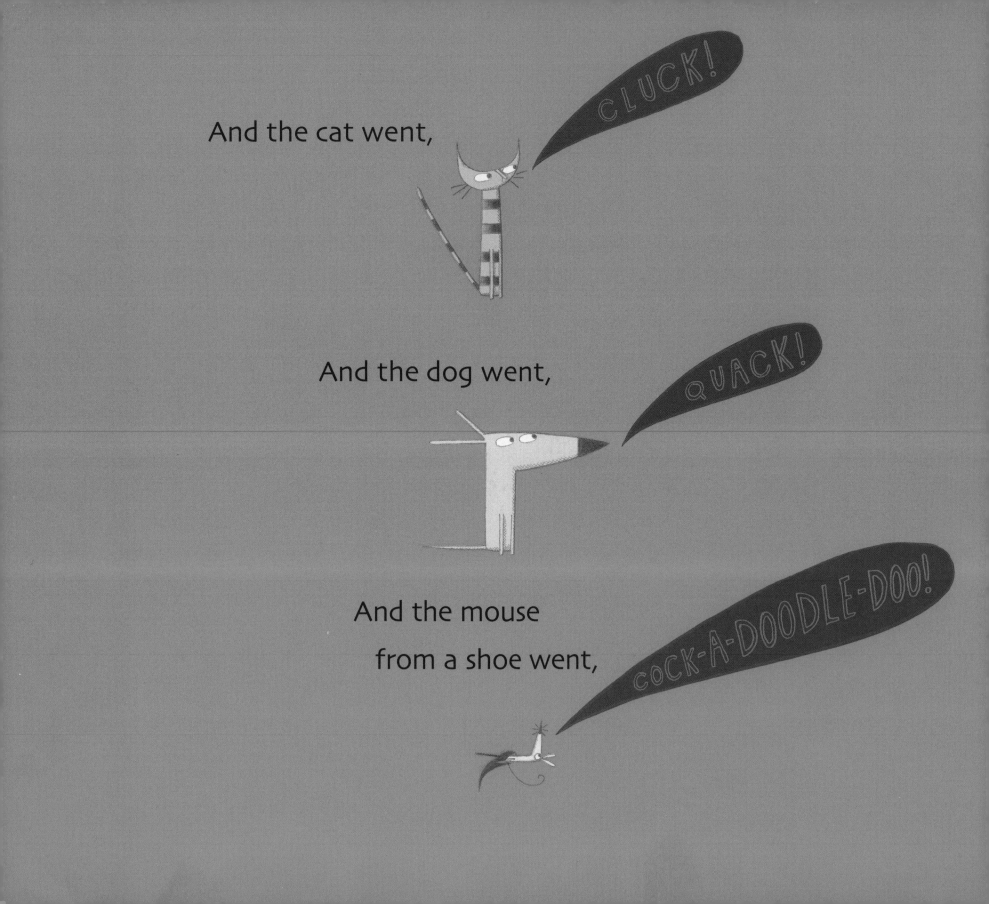

And the little old lady went,

"Oh silly me!
Let's try page three.
That will be the spell
to make you all well."

She went to look at her big spell book.

She cast a spell but the whole house shook.

There was a
FLASH!
And a CRASH!
And a rumbling sound.

And the tumbledown house
turned round and round.

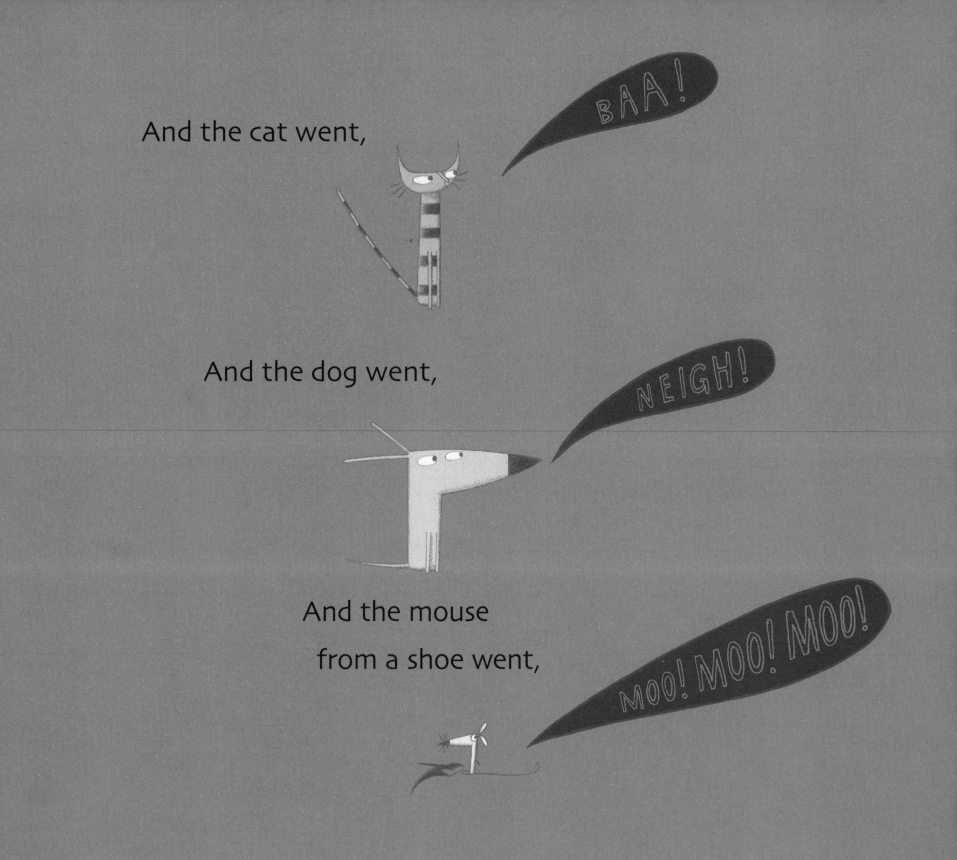

And the little old lady went,

"Oh good heaven!
Shall we try page seven?
That will be the spell
to make you all well."

She went to look at her big spell book.

She cast a spell but the whole house shook.

There was a
BANG!
And a CLANG!
And a thundering sound.

ANd the tumbledown hoUse
turned round and round.

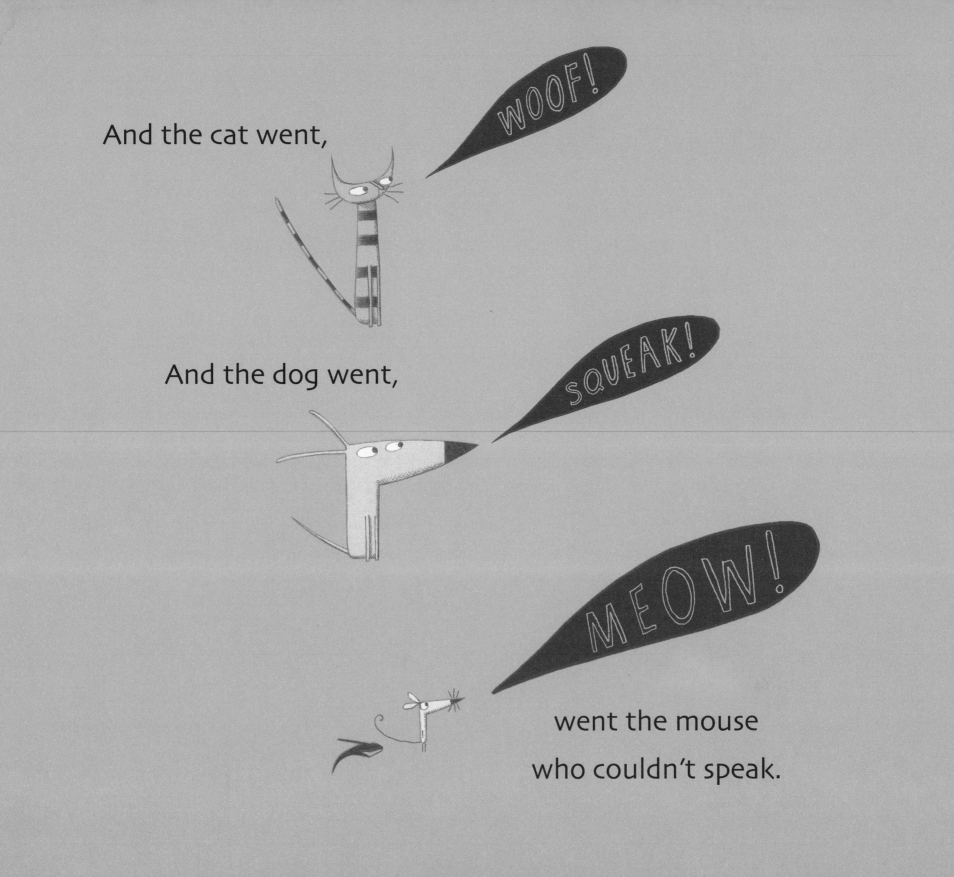

And the little old lady went,

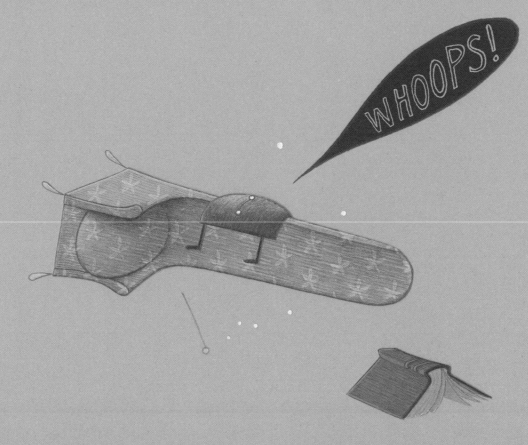

"Oh not again!

Let's try page ten.

This must be the spell

to make you all well."

She went to look
at her big spell book.

She cast a spell
but the whole house shook.

There was a sparkle
and a crackle
and a thundering sound.

There was a FLASH!
And a CRASH!
And a rumbling sound.

And the sky turned brown. The wind blew in.

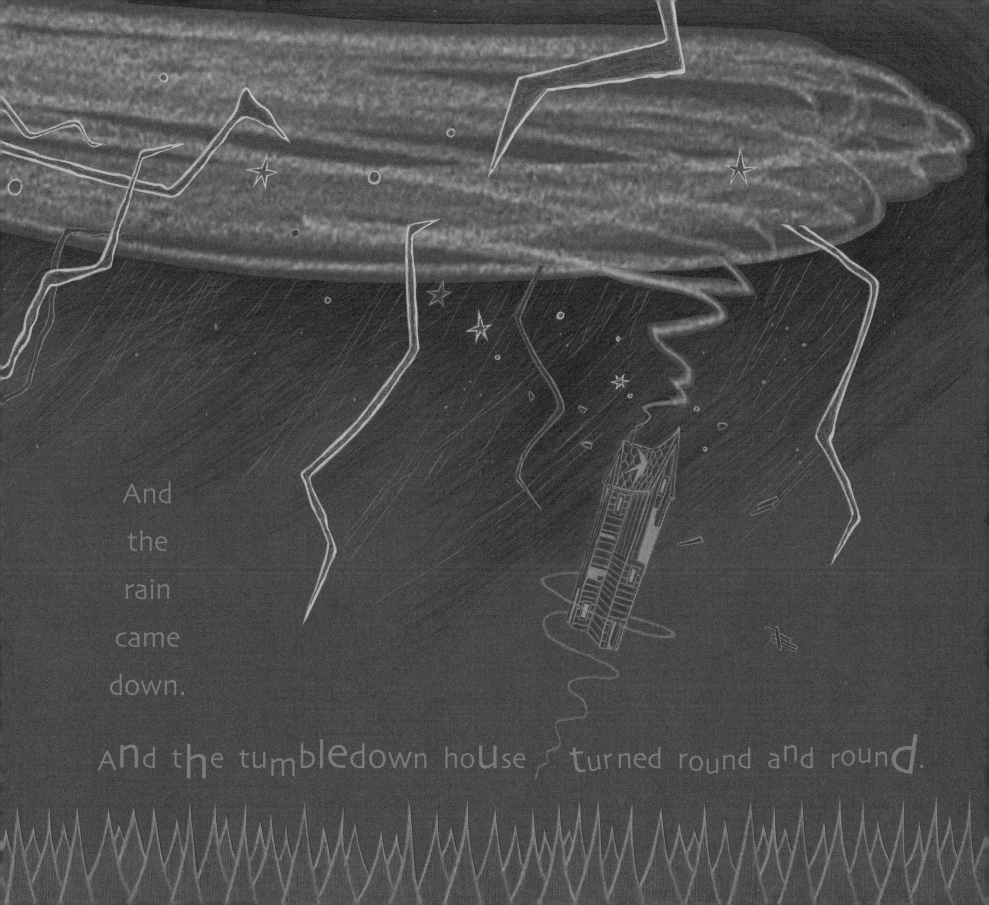

And
the
rain
came
down.

And the tumbledown house turned round and round.

And the cat went,

And the dog went,

The mouse who
couldn't speak went,

And the little old lady went,

And the wise old owl
who was watching from a tree,
looked down with a frown
and he said to the three,

WHOOPS!